Contents

Together *John Kitching* 7

Bounce-a-Ball *Wes Magee* 8

My Friend Sam *Judith Hemington* 10

New Boy *Peter Dixon* 12

Partners *Judith Nicholls* 14

Beside Myself *Gina Douthwaite* 15

Stony *Eric Finney* 16

Haiku *Mike Jubb* 17

Haiku *Tony Bradman* 17

Friends *Tony Bradman* 18

Imaginary Friends *Tony Bradman* 20

Shame *Tracey Blance* 22

Just Friends *Dave Calder* 23

Compulsive Liar *Philip Waddell* 24

What are Friends for? *Patricia Leighton* 26

Finding a Friend *Jane Clarke* 27

Internet Pen-Pal *Andrew Collett* 28

Best Friends *Adrian Henri* 29

My Friend *John Walsh* 30

No Friends *Alethia Walker* 32

New Friends *Damian Gordon* 33

Three Friends *Jane Clarke* 34

Rhoda *Jeff Moss* 36

Poem *Langston Hughes* 38

Wanna Be Your Friend *Paul Bright* 39

My Pal Billy *John Yeoman* 40

Reading to My Friend Miss Cross
    Helen Dunmore   42
I Got Friends *Ivan Jones*   44
Celebration *Frances Nagle*   46
Friends *Benjamin Zephaniah*   47
Pals *Brian Patten*   48
Me and Amanda *Colin West*   49
Latch Key *Jackie Kay*   50
When My Friend Anita Runs
    Grace Nichols   52
Rabbit and Lark *James Reeves*   54
Copycat *Irene Rawnsley*   56
When You Meet Your Friend
    Greek Traditional   58
With Clothes *Chinese Traditional*   58
A Friendship Poem *Roger McGough*   59
Friends *Elizabeth Jennings*   60
Since Hanna Moved Away *Judith Viorst*   61
Tracy Venables *Colin McNaughton*   62

I Wanna Be
Your Mate

I Wanna Be Your Mate

Poems about Friends

Selected by
TONY BRADMAN

Illustrated by
Colin Paine

BLOOMSBURY
CHILDREN'S
BOOKS

For Jackie and Mike – C.P.

First published in Great Britain in 1999
Bloomsbury Publishing Plc, 38 Soho Square, London, W1V 5DF

Individual poem copyright details feature on the acknowledgements
page located at the back of this book
Copyright © Text this selection Tony Bradman 1999
Copyright © Illustrations Colin Paine 1999

The moral right of the author has been asserted
A CIP catalogue record of this book is available from the
British Library

ISBN 0 7475 4451 4

Printed in England by Clays Ltd, St Ives plc

10 9 8 7 6 5 4 3 2 1

Together

We're bacon and eggs.
We're fried fish and chips.
We're curry and rice.
We're lipstick and lips.

We're baked beans on toast.
We're cake and ice-cream.
We're letter and stamp.
We're kettle and steam.

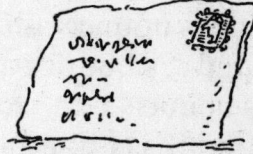

We're water and fish.
We're blanket and bed.
We're saucer and cup.
We're hat and its head.

We're curtain and window.
We're bright shoe and sock.
We're picture and frame.
We're door and strong lock.

We fit well together.
We have no loose ends.
So that's how we know
That we'll always be friends.

John Kitching

Bounce-a-Ball

With my friends at playtime
  I play bounce-a-ball.
    It's bounce-a-ball to Emma
      and it's bounce-a-ball to Paul.
      It's bounce-a-ball to Ahmed
        and it's bounce-a-ball to Faz.
      It's bounce-a-ball to Guljit
      and it's bounce-a-ball to Jazz.
    It's bounce-a-ball to Stacey
  and it's bounce-a-ball to Matt.
It's bounce-a-ball to Sophie
  and it's bounce-a-ball to Pat.
    It's bounce-a-ball to Jeeta
      and it's bounce-a-ball to Luke.
      It's bounce-a-ball to Hannah
        and it's bounce-a-ball to Duke.
      It's bounce-a-ball to Chloe
  and it's bounce-a-ball to Wayne.

It's bounce-a-ball to Amy
and it's bounce-a-ball to Shane.
There goes the school bell
and now our playtime ends.
I played bounce-a-ball

with

my

best

friends.

Hey!

Wes Magee

My Friend Sam

When I bring Sam to our house
It doesn't please my mum.
She doesn't like his toothy grin,
Nor his chewing gum.
Sam's not the sort to say too much,
Not to anyone.
She thinks his grunts are rather rude,
But Sam's a lot of fun.
He always has these great ideas,
Like building dens and things.
He knows about the countryside –
And plants and nettle stings.
When Sam's about, things tend to break –
It's always Sam Mum blames.
She says whenever he's around

We play such rowdy games.
It often isn't all Sam's fault,
But once you've got a name
Even if you're innocent
They blame you all the same.
Sam doesn't seem to mind too much,
Perhaps he's used to it.
When teachers tell him off at school
He doesn't care a bit.
Those Saturdays when Sam turns up
The hours just melt away.
Sam's the kind of friend to have,
Whatever grown-ups say.

Judith Hemington

New Boy

Harry Pigstore – what a laugh!
Harry Pigstore – in our class
Harry Pigstore – what a name
We don't want you in our game.

Harry Pigstore – what a state
We don't want you for our mate!
Harry Pigstore leave him out
Harry Pigstore-snout . . . snout . . . snout

Harry Pigstore – where's your dad?
Drives a Lotus Red-Elan!
Lead guitar in Roxy Mode,
That big house up Bombay Road!

Got three houses – judo star
Brother's got a racing car!
Helicopter for your mum
We're really really glad
– you've come!

Stay and play, be our goalie
Play midfield, instead of Coley
Wanna stay and play tonight?
Stay with us, you'll be all right.

We're your mates
My name's Russ,
Stick around –
Be one of us!

Peter Dixon

Partners

Find a partner,
says sir, and sit
with him or her.
A whisper here,
a shuffle there,
a rush of feet.
One pair,
another pair,
till twenty-four
sit safely on the floor
and all are gone
but one
who stands,
like stone,
and waits;
tall,
still,

alone.

Judith Nicholls

Beside Myself

I'm quite beside myself
you see
I have no better friend
than me.

I won't fall out
nor let me down,
yell nasty names,
spread lies around,

I will not wonder why I swopped
me for another friend,
got dropped

from being best
to being worst,
from being loved
to being cursed

for I can trust me to defend
myself –
I am my own best friend.

Gina Douthwaite

Stony

We found this secret beach
Of sea-smooth stones last year:
What fun we had here!
We flung stones out to sea at first
Over the running tide,
Your lazy throws always the winners
No matter how hard I tried.
Then we bombed blobs of seaweed
With nearly fist-sized stones:
At hits and near misses
Gave cheers or groans.
Then, leaning against two boulders,
Arms round each others shoulders,
We listened to shifting stones
In the tug and suck of the sea;
Last year, you and me.

This year, remembering,
I walked the beach alone
And everything was cold
And grey as stone.

Eric Finney

Haiku

Like a boomerang,
mean words behind your friend's back
can return to you.

Mike Jubb

Haiku

My friend is silent.
In the cloakroom our coats hang
empty, side by side.

Tony Bradman

Friends

I'm only little
You're very big
I eat like a mouse
You eat like a pig

But we're friends, just the same

I like it quiet
You like it LOUD!
I like to be alone sometimes
You're always in a crowd

But we're friends, just the same

I have seven brothers
You've just got your mum
You're not afraid of anything
I still suck my thumb

But we're friends, just the same

I'm good with numbers
You're good with words
I don't know any funny jokes
Yours are the best I've heard

But we're friends, just the same

People think it's funny
They think we're very strange
They say it won't be very long
Before our feelings change

But we're friends, just the same

Tony Bradman

Imaginary Friends

I have a friend
Who isn't there
In fact she isn't
Anywhere

My friend's imaginary
Or so Mum says
And yet I see her
Every day

She sits right next
To me at tea
And also when
I watch TV

She sleeps beside me
In my bed
But my mum says
She's in my head

My friend says
That it's okay
She doesn't mind
What Mum says

But ssshhh . . . this is secret!
Between you and me
My friend thinks it's *Mum*
Who's imaginary

Tony Bradman

Shame

There's a girl at school
we teased today;
made jokes, called her names.
My friends all laughed,
called it harmless fun,
said it was just a game.

Now I'm at home
feeling horrid inside,
long gone that thoughtless grin.
How will I face her
tomorrow at school?
I wish I hadn't joined in.

Tracey Blance

Just Friends

Me and my friend
crawl though bushes to secret dens,
climb trees and walls,
play football.

My friend can flatten big boys with a shove
or stand like a rock and shout them down.
When we're together we're stronger than two
life's more fun with my friend around.

Me and my friend
don't have to pose or pretend:
there's nothing between us
but trust.

Yet the stupid sniggers are painful,
and silly gestures make me sore –
why can't a boy and girl be friends,
just friends, nothing more?

Dave Calder

Compulsive Liar

My best friend tells lies all the time.
He says he's lost his homework
when he hasn't even done it.
He says he's feeling sick
when he wants to bunk off school.
I've even heard him lie about his name –
when we got caught scrumping apples one
    time.
My friend is such a liar that he'll even lie
for absolutely no reason at all.
For example if you ask him,
'Do you like chocolate ice-cream?'
which everyone knows he's crazy about,
he'll automatically say, 'No, I hate it.'

My dad says, 'That boy's a compulsive liar,'
which means that it's so natural
for him to tell lies that he can't help it.
But yesterday something happened
which I believe shows that there is some hope
   for him.
Our teacher asked him who, in his opinion,
was the smartest pupil in the school.
Quick as a flash he pointed at me and said,
   'He is.'
I don't know why everyone laughed.

Philip Waddell

What are Friends for?

Leroy gave me
  half his Mars bar
Leroy shared
  a can of Coke
Leroy let me
  use his Gameboy
When mine broke

Leroy let me
  be in his gang
Leroy shared
  his favourite joke
Leroy gave me
  his best conker
And his Batman cloak.

Leroy says
  I am the greatest
Leroy says
  I am the tops
Leroy's had
  two weeks off school 'cos
I gave Leroy chickenpox!

Patricia Leighton

Finding a Friend

I could not speak your language.
I did not know your rules.
Everything felt foreign
to an alien at school.

Those days are long gone now,
though I thought they'd never end.
Now I have no problems
speaking English, making friends.

Dark and haunting memories
of loneliness and fear,
frustration and confusion
have begun to disappear.

But one thing I'll remember,
one thing will stay the same.
The moment that you smiled at me
and called me by my name.

Jane Clarke

Internet Pen-Pal

I've never called at his house
or heard his real name,
I have to guess at his voice
for they all sound the same.

I've never been round for tea
or stayed there all night,
I don't know if he's small
or towering in height.

But when we both talk
see the smile on my face,
for he's my best friend
in all of cyberspace.

Andrew Collett

Best Friends

It's Susan I talk to not Tracey,
Before that I sat next to Jane;
I used to be best friends with Lynda
But these days I think she's a pain.

Natasha's all right in small doses,
I meet Mandy sometimes in town;
I'm jealous of Annabel's pony
And I don't like Nicola's frown.

I used to go skating with Catherine,
Before that I went there with Ruth;
And Kate's so much better at trampoline:
She's a show-off, to tell you the truth.

I think that I'm going off Susan,
She borrowed my comb yesterday;
I *think* I might sit next to Tracey,
She's my nearly best friend: she's okay.

Adrian Henri

My Friend

I don't like her any more
she threw my friend out of our house
and won't let him back in

She said
it was because of the way he ate his food
and that he made a mess everywhere
and treated our house
as if it were his own

She was very annoyed
when he walked into her bedroom
and even more annoyed when she found him
    asleep in the bath
and boy was she mad
when she caught him going into the fridge

She said that was the last straw
and threw him out

I bet I'll never see him again now

She's mean!
she didn't like him because he was different

She says there must be something wrong with
   me
for wanting him as a friend
but I don't think so

I bet there's lots of people
who have cockroaches as friends

John Walsh

No Friends

I have got no friends –
I can't ask anyone if they
Will lend me felt-tip pens,
There is a girl across the
Table who has got a horse
And stable,
I know all these things
Because I hear her talking.
I am all alone on my table.

Every day when I watch them play,
I don't understand what they say,
They won't let me join in,
I stay in locked away,
My mum and dad say go out,
It is a nice day,
But if I haven't got
Any friends
            I can't.

Alethia Walker, 10

New Friends

At my last school
I played in the Lego
with Sumwa.

Now I am
in a different school
playing with Nathan and Dwayne.

They are my friends now.

In my old school,
do they think I am on holiday?

But I told Mrs Jessingham.
I told it loud
so Sumwa might know
where I am.

Sumwa will be playing in the Lego
with Iqubal now.

Damian Gordon, 6

Three Friends

Kento and Khalil and me,
we're a trio, we are three.
As close as any friends can be.

Life is awesome, life is fun.
I'd rather have two friends than one.

Kento says that I look dumb
when I sit and suck my thumb.
I don't care what Kento thinks.
Khalil's my best friend. Kento stinks.

Life's all right, life's okay.
One friend is enough today.

Khalil says Kento's not so bad.
He likes Kento. I get mad.
Kento and Khalil agree
that it's time to pick on me.

Life is lonely, life is blue
when your friends gang up on you.

Kento and Khalil fall out.
Our threesome is what it's about.
We know our friendship's on the line.
Can we make it up this time?

Life is perfect, life is great.
The three of us are best of mates.

Though we often disagree,
three friends we are meant to be,
Kento and Khalil and me.

Jane Clarke

Rhoda

My friend Rhoda is always very *busy*.
She is always *moving*.
She does everything *fast*.

You can never say to Rhoda, 'Hey, look at that
    pretty flower,'
because Rhoda has already run *past* it.

You cannot say to Rhoda, 'Look at that weird
    puffy cloud
that's shaped like a goldfish,'
Because if she looked up at the sky, Rhoda
    wouldn't be
able to watch where she was *running*.

Even when she washes dishes or sets the table
    or gets
dressed or reads a poem, Rhoda does it *fast*.

It's hard to just sit around and have a chat
    with her.

But if you want to have a race or double-jump
    rope or see how
quick you can change into your pyjamas,
Rhoda is a great friend to have.

And, after all, there are other friends
to do slow things with.

Jeff Moss

Poem

I loved my friend.
He went away from me.
There's nothing more to say.
The poem ends,
Soft as it began –
I loved my friend:

Langston Hughes

Wanna Be Your Friend

Hi there! I wanna be your friend
We could go down town, can you maybe lend
Me a pound or two till the end of the week
Hey is that your mum? What a real antique.

Hi there! I wanna be your mate
Can I borrow your bike, or I'm gonna be late?
It's a bit of a wreck! But it'll have to do
Is that fruit and nut? Guess I'll have some too!

Hi there! I wanna be your buddy
How about some fun. Do you have to study?
Throw away your pen. You don't need that
    book
Is that Tuesday's maths? Let me take a look!

Hi there! I wanna be your friend
I've been through my list, now I'm at the end
I can't find no friends, and I don't know why
When I'm such a wonderful kind of guy

Paul Bright

My Pal Billy

My pal Billy has a first-rate mind;
His marks in History leave us way behind;
He's best in reading; he's a whizz at sums
(And he gives the answers out to all his
    chums).

But don't think Billy's only top in class:
He's an ace at soccer (you should see him
    pass).
And when the break arrives he looks so proud
As he puts a show on for the waiting crowd:

It's acrobatics, any time you like,
On his roller-blades or on his mountain bike.
He can juggle apples; he can make you laugh;
He can tie a Sheepshank in his old school
    scarf;

He's a champ at wrestling; he can swallow
    fire;
He can do a somersault, or change your tyre;
He can leave you baffled with a conjuring
    trick –

My pal Billy really makes me sick.

John Yeoman

Reading to My Friend Miss Cross

Miss Cross next door
is thin as paper
and the wind aches her.
After school I read to her.

'Tuck my shawl in tight,' she tells me.
We suck Fox's Glacier Mints,
drink our tea, then begin
on the front page with the headlines.

'Well,' she says, *'would you believe it?*
Such wickedness!' Then I turn
the pages and read the horoscope
and tonight's TV programmes.

It's hard work, reading
all the big words and long columns
but Miss Cross says
the way I read, she can just see it.

Miss Cross wears a woolly hat
indoors, to keep her head warm.
She wraps her scarf around her
like a snowman in the garden.

She is thin as paper
and her bones ache her,
but we tuck her shawl in tight
and she says when I'm reading to her
she always feels warm.

Helen Dunmore

I Got Friends

I got friends of many races
I got friends in many places
I got friends with funny faces
   I got friends

I got friends with double chins
I got friends as thin as tins
I got friends with spotty skins
   I got friends

I got friends who live in rooms
I got friends who hang round tombs
I got friends who like to groom
   I got friends

I got friends who look like Dracula
I got friends who look spectacular
I got friends who speak vernacular
   I got friends

I got friends that love computers
I got friends who are commuters
I got friends who ride on scooters
   I got friends

The good, the bad, the ugly
The trim, the dim, the muddly
Whoever they are, they're cuddly!
   I got friends!

Ivan Jones

Celebration

When I get the ball
I whizz down the wing,
Dribble it past
The opposing team,
Cross to our striker,
My best mate Joel,
And whoopee –
It's a goal.

Then . . .
Hell for leather
We race towards each other
CLASH our wheelchairs together.

Frances Nagle

Friends

Funky monkey in the tree
I like when you talk to me
What I really like the best
Is when you bang upon my chest.

Slippery snake I am your mate
When all others hesitate
I'll be there right by your side
I am known to slip and slide.

Hop along, croak croak, how ya doing **frog?**
No one understands our deep dialogue
People may laugh when they see us on the
    road
We must stick together
Monkey, snake, me, you and **toad**.

Benjamin Zephaniah

Pals

I'm sorry for shouting.
Let's be pals.
I was wrong the other day.
All those months of being friends I've startled
   away.
Like a flock of frightened birds.

Brian Patten

Me and Amanda

Me
and
Amanda
meander
like
rivers
that
run
to
the
sea.
We
wander
at
random
we're
always
in
tandem:
meandering
Mandy
and
me.

Colin West

Latch Key

My best friend Danny comes to dinner with a
    key
round his neck, tied on with a piece of string.
At night when no one's home he lets himself
    in,
even though he is only seven, only seven.
My mum says he's too young and it's a
    shame.
He watches TV alone and eats crisps left for
    him.
And Mrs Robinson – the old woman next
    door –
listens out for him. Though my mum says
she is hard of hearing. What does that mean?

Danny's mummy is always rushing off
    somewhere,
all dressed up to the nines and sometimes,
when the taxi comes she throws a kiss
like a piece of bread to a duck; it drops on our
    street
with a sigh. Then Danny scoops up his kiss
and comes into our house holding on to it.
Can Danny have a bath with me? I plead,
and my mum sighs yes, she supposes so,
because he is only seven, only seven.

Jackie Kay

When My Friend Anita Runs

When my friend Anita runs
She runs straight into the headalong –
legs flashing over grass, daisies, mounds.

When my friend Anita runs
she sticks out her chest like an Olympic
champion – face all serious concentration.

And you'll never catch her looking around,
until she flies into the invisible tape
that says, she's won.

Then she turns to give me
this big grin and hug

O to be able to run like Anita,
                     run like Anita,
Who runs like a cheetah.
If only, just for once, I could beat her.

Grace Nichols

Rabbit and Lark

'Under the ground
    It's rumbly and dark
And interesting,'
    Said Rabbit to Lark.

Said Lark to Rabbit,
    'Up in the sky
There's plenty of room
    And it's airy and high.'

'Under the ground
    It's warm and dry.
Won't you live with me?'
    Was Rabbit's reply.

'The air's so sunny.
    I wish you'd agree,'
Said the little Lark,
    'To live with me.'

But under the ground
    And up in the sky,
Larks can't burrow
    Nor rabbits fly.

So Skylark over
   And Rabbit under
They had to settle
   To live asunder.

And often these two friends
   Meet with a will
For a chat together
   On top of the hill.

James Reeves

Copycat

Every time we have painting
Jonathan copies me.

Today I did a red house
with a chimney on top,
made smoke come out,
put curtains at the window,
a cat on the doorstep,
a tree in the garden
with one blackbird,
a path, a gate,
and a big sun shining.

When I looked at his picture
Jonathan had copied me

He had a red house,
a smoking chimney,
a cat on the doorstep,
curtains at the window,
a garden, a tree
with a blackbird perched
on the same branch,
a path leading to a gate
and a big sun shining.

The teacher said, 'Which of you copied?'
But I didn't tell.
Jonathan's a copycat
but he's my friend as well.

Irene Rawnsley

When You Meet Your Friend

When you meet your friend,
your face brightens –
you have struck gold.

Kassia, 9th Century
Greece

With Clothes

With clothes the new are best:
with friends the old are best.

Traditional
China

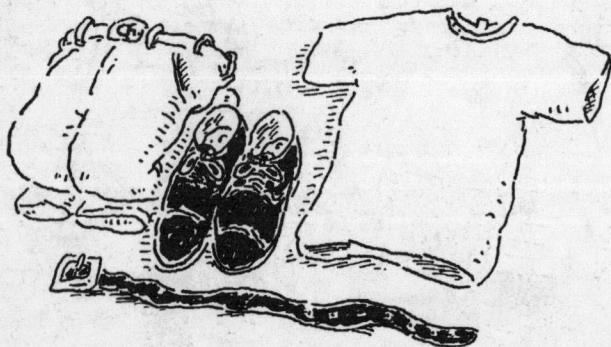

A Friendship Poem

There's good mates and bad mates
   'Sorry to keep you waiting' mates
Cheap skates and wet mates
   The ones you end up hating mates
Hard mates and fighting mates
   Witty and exciting mates
Mates you want to hug
   And mates you want to clout
Ones that get you into trouble
   And ones that get you out.

Roger McGough

Friends

I fear it's very wrong of me,
And yet I must admit,
When someone offers friendship
I want the *whole* of it.
I don't want everybody else
To share my friends with me.
At least, I want *one* special one
Who, indisputably,

Likes me much more than all the rest,
Who's always on my side,
Who never cares what others say,
Who lets me come and hide
Within his shadow, in his house –
It doesn't matter where –
Who lets me simply be myself,
Who's always, *always* there.

Elizabeth Jennings

Since Hanna Moved Away

The tyres on my bike are flat.
The sky is grouchy grey.
At least it sure feels like that
Since Hanna moved away.

Chocolate ice-cream tastes like prunes.
December's come to stay.
They've taken back the Mays and Junes
Since Hanna moved away.

Flowers smell like halibut.
Velvet feels like hay.
Every handsome dog's a mutt
Since Hanna moved away.

Nothing's fun to laugh about.
Nothing's fun to play.
They call me, but I won't come out
Since Hanna moved away.

Judith Viorst

Tracy Venables

Tracy Venables thinks she's great,
Swinging on her garden gate.
She's the girl I love to hate –
'Show-off' Tracy Venables.

She's so fat she makes me sick,
Eating ice-cream, lick, lick, lick.
I know where I'd like to kick
'Stink-pot' Tracy Venables.

Now she's shouting 'cross the street,
What's she want, the dirty cheat?
Would I like some? Oh, how sweet
Of my friend Tracy Venables.

Colin McNaughton

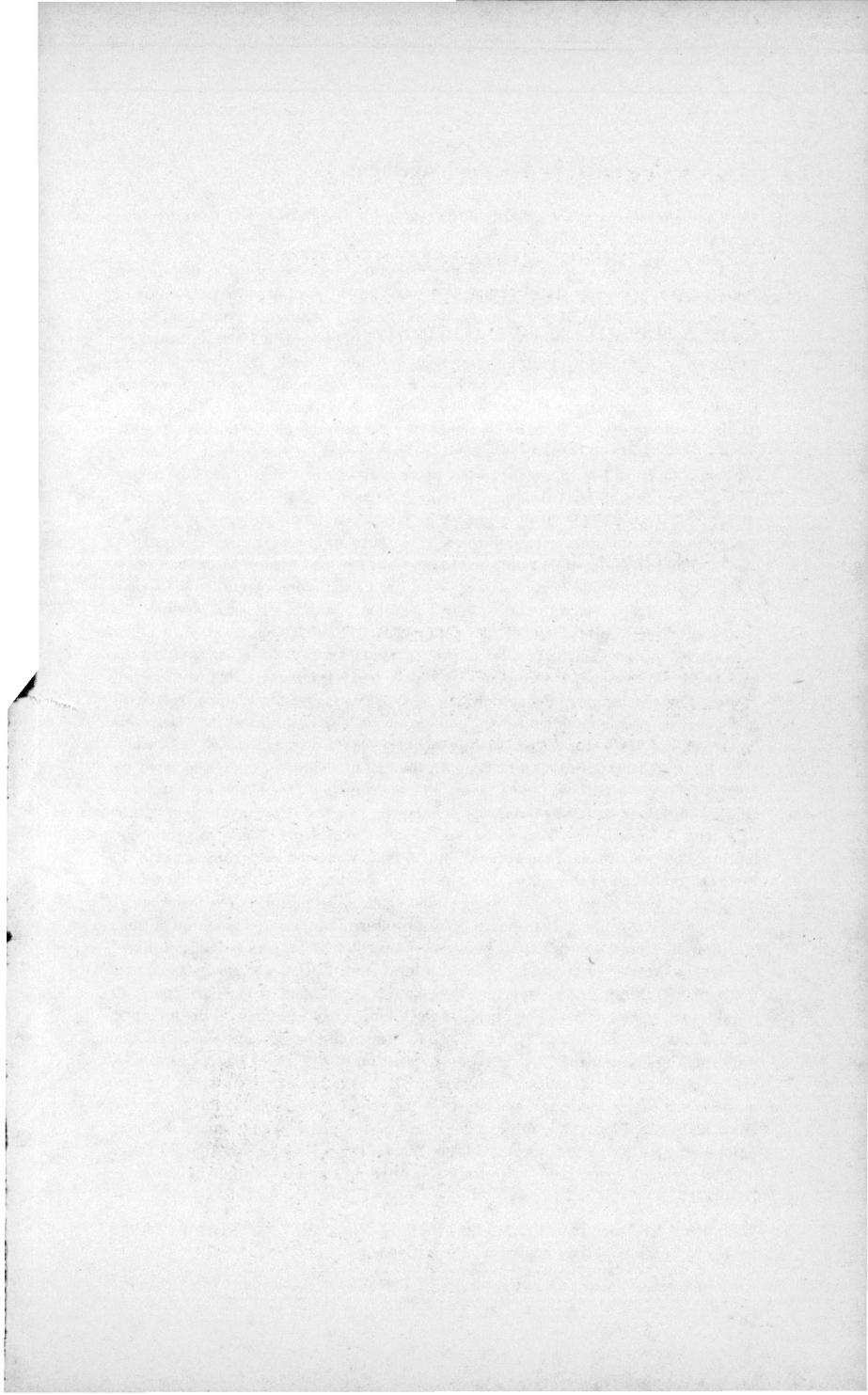

Acknowledgements

The Publishers gratefully acknowledge the following permission to reproduce copyright material in this book.

'Together' copyright © John Kitcling 1999, reprinted by permission of the author; 'Bounce-a-Ball' copyright © the author, Wes Magee 1999. Reprinted by permission of the author; 'My Friend Sam' reprinted by permission of Laurence Pollinger Ltd on behalf of Judith Hemington; 'New Boy' from Cool published in 1999, reprinted by permission of the author; 'Partners' copyright © Judith Nicholls 1987, from *Midnight Forest* by Judith Nicholls, published by Faber & Faber. Reprinted by permission of the author; 'Stony' copyright © Eric Finney, reprinted by permission of the author; 'Haiku' copyright © Mike Jubb, reprinted by permission of the author; 'Haiku' copyright © Tony Bradman, reprinted by permission of the author; 'Friends' copyright © Tony Bradman, reprinted by permission of the author; 'Imaginary Friends' copyright © Tony Bradman, reprinted by permission of the author; 'Shame' copyright © Tracey Blance 1999, reprinted by permission of the author; 'Just Friends' copyright © Dave Calder 1998, reprinted by permission of the author; 'Compulsive Liar' by Philip Waddell (first published in *My Gang* by Brian Moses, Macmillan 1999) reprinted by permission of the author; 'What are Friends for?' copyright © Patricia Leighton 1999, reprinted by permission of the author; 'Finding a Friend' reprinted by permission of the author, Jane Clarke; 'Internet Pen-Pal' reprinted by permission of the author, Andrew Collett; 'Best Friends' © Adrian Henri 1998, from *The World's Your Lobster* by Adrian Henri, published by Bloomsbury Publishing Plc; My Friend' reprinted by permission of the author, John Walsh; 'No Friends' by Alethia Walker, 10 (p.88, 18 lines) and 'New Friends' by Damian Gordon, 6 (p.77, 15 lines) from *Letter to a Friend* (Puffin, 1989) Copyright (Alethia Walker, 1989, Copyright (Damian Gordon, 1989. Reprinted by permission of Penguin Books Ltd; 'Three Friends' reprinted by permission of the author, Jane Clarke; 'Poem' from *Collected Poems* by Langston Hughes copyright © 1994 by the Estate of Langston Hughes. Reprinted by permission of Alfred A Knopf Inc.; 'Wanna Be Your Friend' copyright © Paul Bright 1999, reprinted by permission of the author; 'My Pal Billy' reprinted by permission of A. P. Watt Ltd on behalf of the author, John Yeoman; 'Reading to My Friend Miss Cross' reprinted by permission of A. P. Watt Ltd on behalf of the author, Helen Dunmore; 'I Got Friends' copyright © Ivan Jones 1999, reproduced by permission of the author; 'Celebration' from You can't call a hedgehog Hopscotch by Frances Nagle, published by Dagger Press 1999; 'Friends' (p.22, 13 Lines) from *Talking Turkeys* by Benjamin Zephaniah (Viking, 1994) Copyright © Benjamin Zephaniah, 1994; 'Pals' (p.62, 10 lines) from *Gargling with Jelly* by Brian Patten (Viking, 1985) Copyright © Brian Patten, 1985; 'Rabbit and Lark' copyright © James Reeves from *Complete Poems for Children*, published by Heinemann. Reprinted by permission of the James Reeves Estate; 'A Friendship Poem' reprinted by permission of The Peters Fraser & Dunlop Group Ltd on behalf of Roger McGough as printed in the original volume; 'Friends' from *The Secret Brother* by Elizabeth Jennings published by Macmillan; 'Tracy Venables' text of Tracy Venables from *There's an Awful Lot of Weirdos in our Neighbourhood* © 1987 Colin McNaughton. Reproduced by permission of the publisher Walker Books Ltd., London.

Every effort has been made to trace the copyright holders. The publishers would like to hear from any copyright holder not acknowledged.